Summer Blast

Karen Ligocki

ISBN: 978-1-963017-54-0 (Paperback)

Printed in the United Stated of America

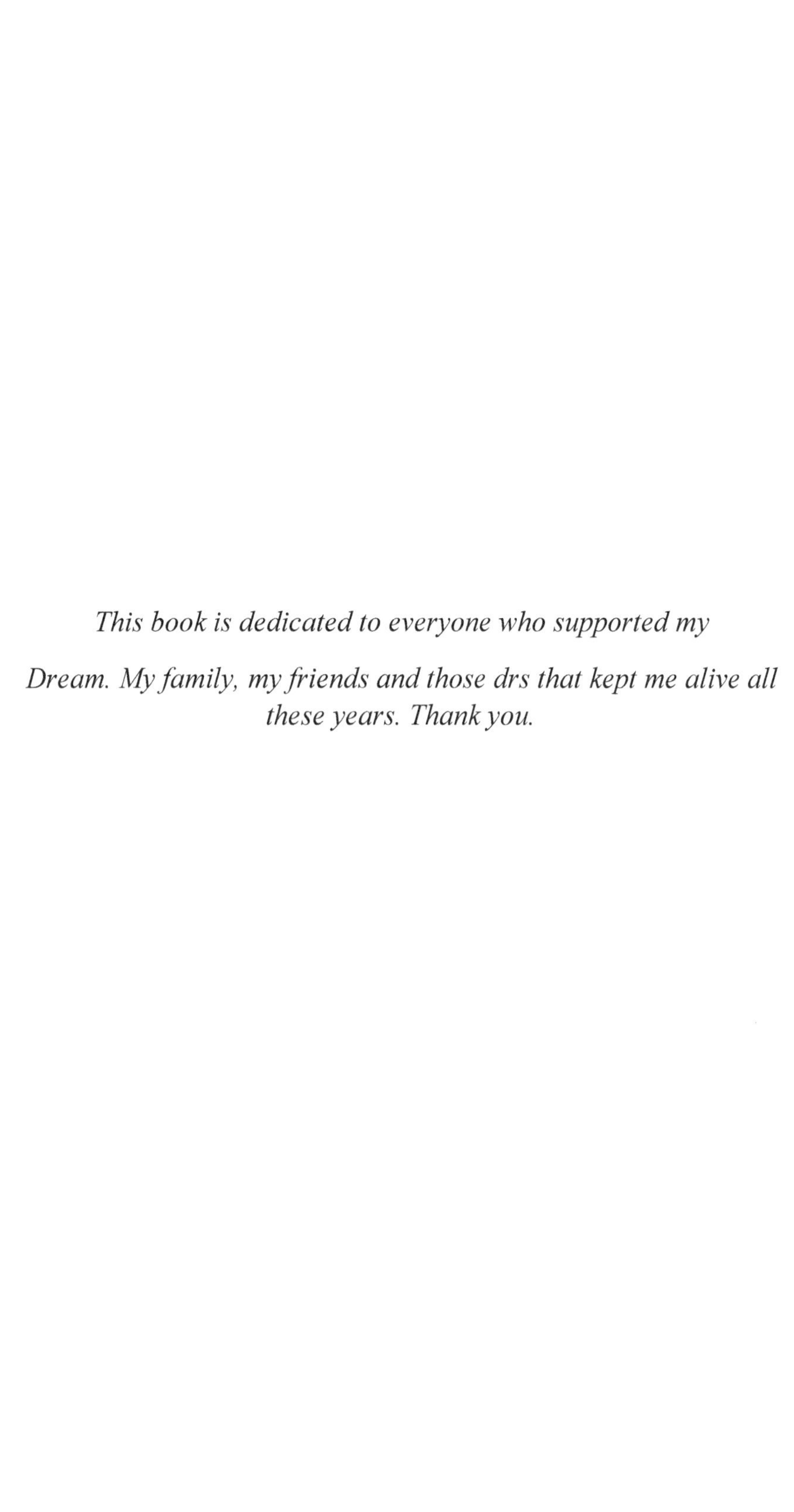

This book is dedicated to everyone who supported my

Dream. My family, my friends and those drs that kept me alive all
these years. Thank you.

Contents

Chapter 1

Paul Wiseman was a young, fit 58 years old. Paul went into the service right after high school. In the academy, he spent the next 20 years rising up through the ranks as a Minneapolis police officer. During this time, he married his high school sweetheart, and they had two boys and a girl. Paul loved being a police officer. He was happy, life was good, and he became Captain in his 15th year. One day, his wife Jessica came to him and told him, "We have to talk Paul." Paul was beside himself. Jessica told him she had stage 4 breast cancer. They vowed to fight. Paul took furlough and was there for every test and chemo, radiation treatment, and crying, but in the end, it didn't help.

Jessica passed away. Paul thought his life had ended as well, or he wanted it to end.

Hours turned into days, days turned into weeks, weeks turned into months, and the one-year anniversary of Jessica's death almost destroyed Paul. He could think of nothing else but the love he lost. Paul's daughter Dorie moved in for a while with her husband Scott and three kids. Everyone thought that having his grandkids around would take him out of his depression.

Once again, Paul had to go on leave from his job, this time a medical leave. The police department paid him to seek help with depression. His status as captain depended on quick, solid decisions. He could not risk his team's lives. Paul agreed to the leave and the medical treatment, only hoping that it would help.

As time went by, Paul learned to handle the grief better, the anxiety and depression lessened, and he was pretty much back to his old self. Pretty much!

The kids kept him busy. He babysat them so Dorie could do some part-time work and get the stuff she needed. Scott was a police lieutenant, but in the city, they moved from, his commute was the worst part of his day.

Paul hit the gym at the station every day. Exercise freed his mind, not letting it go to bad places. Bad places. Bad places weren't all that bad. Paul thought of Jessica and how they were supposed to travel around the world. When he reached 20 years on the force, he would retire and off they'd go. Bad places were just memories of when he and Jessica met, dated, married, and had kids, how these moments in time stuck in his head. Bad places weren't bad. They just hurt after he was done thinking of them.

Paul's return to work went fluently. The captain that covered him was cut from the same cloth. As time passed, Paul couldn't help but feel empty, and the job became like working in a well-oiled machine.

The next month was torture: the job, going home to the house where he made his life with Jessica.

Paul called his oldest son, Jesse.

He already had some things in motion. He wanted to run by Jess, not wanting to upset his son's life. He told Jesse he was thinking about leaving Minnesota. There was silence on the line.

"Jess?" said Paul.

"You're going to sell the house?" Jesse asked.

"Oh no, I thought Dorie and Scott could live there in my absence," Paul clarified.

"Oh!" replied Jesse.

"Does that bother you, son?" Paul asked.

"Of course not, Dad. Now I'm thinking, where is he going?" said Jesse.

"Scott passed the captain's test. I'm going to see if he is approved to take over for me," added Paul.

The conversation was taken by silence for a bit.

"Jesse, would it bother you if I moved to Maine? I'd get myself a little shack and it doesn't even have to be near Poland. ME... I can look near the coast. I'm going to apply to the state police. I just don't want you to feel, I don't know, cramped about me being around." Paul explained.

Jesse didn't leave Minnesota because of his father. He went to college in Boston, and there were trips to Maine after law school, knowing good and well that he did not want to be a lawyer. He applied for the Poland, Maine's Sheriff's dept, then Sheriff.

"Well, Jesse, say something," Paul continued.

Jesse laughed.

"You think you are going to cramp my style?" replied Jesse.

"Not everyone wants their father around," Paul answered.

"Not everyone has you for father. Dad, you are not going to live in a shack. You are going to come live with me," Jesse suggested.

It was Paul's turn to be silent.

"Unless you think I'll cramp your style, Dad," Jesse added.

"Shaddup!" said Paul.

That was almost two years ago, and Paul never regretted his Dad's move.

Chapter 2

Paul looked in the mirror, and all he could think was, why's that old man looking at me? Looking good, healthy, and fit…oh, but those gray hairs played on Paul's mind. I may be getting up in age, but I still want to look my best. Paul had been seeing Jesse's deputy, Lynne Gordon, since the Spring Fling. She was in her late 40s but didn't look older than 30, which made him kind of self-conscious.

Will you look at the time? I am going to be late for work because I'm worried about my looks. Rushing now, Paul almost forgot his gun belt. Way to go, Paul.

"Dad?" said Jesse.

"Talk later, Jesse, I'm late," Paul replied.

Paul got into the station in time, and he went into the briefing room.

His lieutenant came over.

"Hey Wiseman, I have a favor to ask of you," said the lieutenant.

"Sure, Liu, what's up?" asked Paul.

"Take a bike out today. We are short a man in that department," instructed the lieutenant.

Paul did like riding a motorcycle, his motorcycle. Somehow, I'm not going to get out of this. I might well say okay.

"Yeah, sure," Paul replied.

The day went pretty uneventful, with few pullovers. Of course, it only takes one bad driver, a drunk tourist, or a combination of both.

In a split second, one car bounced off the other and the other clipped Paul's back wheel. Paul flew off the bike. Fortunately, he was not in a fast-moving lane. Drivers braked all around Paul, and he rolled into a ball, praying really hard no one would smush him into the asphalt. Suddenly, laughing at the image of a crime scene, his outline would be a round ball. It got so quiet that Paul thought he had died, then suddenly he heard choppers overhead, sirens blaring, and a moment later, a familiar voice.

"PAUL!"

The voice strained and scared. Paul could hear it but couldn't talk. I'm really dead, Steve's gonna find me, I'm gonna be dead. Steven Lin was Paul's first friend when he joined the Maine State Police from Michigan.

"PAUL!"

Paul managed to groan out, "Steve?" It was nothing more than a whisper.

"OMG! He's over here. Paul, Paul, look at me."

Paul opened his eyes, he tried to smile, but it hurt. The medics ran over, and a young female medic named Lisa checked Paul's pupils.

"Hello in there," said Lisa.

Paul breathed out a hi.

"Did you cause all of this commotion? I was just about to take my meal?" continued Lisa.

Paul smiled.

"What's your name, Big guy?" added Lisa.

Paul went to sit up and said, "Paul."

"Alright, Paul, just lay back down. Let me and my partner do our job. We are going to get you to the hospital and let them check you out," said Lisa.

Doesn't look like anything's broken, but you were thrown about 100 ft." To Steve, Lisa said.

"We are going to transport and I think he's okay, but bruised and shaken up. We are going to Central, will you meet us?" asked Lisa.

"Yeah, I am off shift now. I'll be there. I'm Steve," replied Steve, "Lisa. I'll see you there."

Paul croaked, "I'm dying over here, and you are picking up the medic, Lin."

Lisa and Steve laughed, and the male medic Oliver laughed, too.

"Let's go, Lis." The medics loaded Paul up, and he looked over to see the motorcycle that he was riding being loaded on a flatbed. Oliver saw him looking.

"You know, Mr Wiseman, it was actually a blessing. You were thrown from that bike, it would have been much worse," said Oliver.

"Yeah, I can see that," replied Paul.

Lisa chimed in.

"Hopefully, they will patch you up and be on your way," Oliver said to Paul.

"She single, for my friend, not me?" exclaimed Paul.

Oliver laughed and said in a loud voice, "Sir, you know, I cannot give out the relationship status of a coworker."

"I'm single, Mr. Wiseman, and your friend is adorable, even panic-stricken," continued Paul. "So, when Lin messes things up, the backup plan is I want to invite you both to Poland's Summer Blast on the 3rd of July. I hope you're not on shift."

Oliver looked at Lisa and nodded, "We'll be there."

Chapter 3

The doctors checked Paul out and decided he needed to stay overnight, precautionary because he had a goose egg lump on his noggin. He wished they'd stop asking him questions, though. If they asked him one more time what year it was, he's going to say 1980.

They took more labs from Paul, and the Doctors told him again that everything looked good. Then, his lieutenant came in with a few of his fellow officers. Lin had left a little while ago and said he'd be back tonight with some coffee.

"Paul, I'm sorry I put you out there. I should have gotten a floater," said the lieutenant.

"Adam, I'm fine. Truthfully, you don't know how a less experienced rider would have turned out. I felt the clip and knew how to react," replied Paul.

"Dad!" Jesse ran into the room, followed by Lynne.

"Paul, I'll talk to you tomorrow," said Adam.

Adam nodded at Jesse and Lynne. Jesse waited for the goodbyes and till the guys left.

"What were you thinking?" asked Jesse.

"Jess..." Paul said.

"No, I know you are a grown man, but I thought when you moved here... why were you on a motorcycle?" continued Jesse.

Lynne held Paul's hand.

"Honey, I have to agree with Jesse, a motorcycle?" said Lynne.

"They were short-handed. I'm an experienced rider. Give me credit," Paul replied.

Jesse sighed a long, weary sigh.

"I know Dad, but believe it or not, nobody from your unit contacted us. Steve called us a little while ago, asking us how we are holding up. Imagine my frustration when he told me what happened. We couldn't get here any faster," Jesse complained.

"I'm sorry, Son," apologized Paul.

"It's okay. We just got a little shaken. What's the Drs. saying?" inquired Jesse.

"They said I could take my bike out tomorrow," replied Paul.

Jesse laughed, and Lynne swatted Paul's shoulder.

"You are a brat." Jesse and Lynne made sure Paul was okay after supper, then headed out.

"I'll drop by to pick you up tomorrow, Dad," informed Jesse.

"Okay," answered Paul. Jesse and Lynne passed Steve in the lobby.

"How's the patient?" asked Steve.

"As hilarious as ever," Paul added.

"That's our boy," responded Steve.

"Steve, thanks for letting us know. We'd still be waiting for him to come home," said Jesse.

"I'm kinda surprised, Jesse. That's the first thing you would have thought that someone from the station, you know, should have notified you," added Steve.

"Well, he's okay, so it's fine. I'm going to come get him in the morning, stop by the house tomorrow, Steve," Jesse added.

"Sounds like a plan. See you two tomorrow," responded Steve.

Steve walked into Paul's room. He started reminiscing when Paul first showed up from Minnesota. Steve remembered his first judgment of his friend.

Jerk, Steve thought, look at this guy, not friendly at all, so full of himself. Steve steered clear of Paul for about those first two weeks, then one day, Paul pulled his cruiser alongside Steve's.

"Hey Lin, did I do something to offend you?" asked Paul.

"No, I mean, I just figured you were.. mean," Lin replied.

Paul laughed so hard he spilled coffee on himself. That was the start of their friendship. Coming back to reality, Steve walked up to Paul's bed and asked, "Where's my coffee?"

"Me, me, me. Here. What stations do you get on this TV."

"Medical shows! "

Thank God Paul was okay. Steve needed him more than he knew.

"Did you ask the pretty medic out? What was her name? Oliver?" Steve laughed.

"Lisa! And no, I lost my nerve," said Paul.

Steve stared at Paul.

"I know, I know. Maybe I'll run into her again someday," continued Paul.

I know you will, Paul thought to himself. I know you will. They watched some TV, drank coffee, and talked until visiting hours were over. "I'll be by your house tomorrow. Jesse has invited me," said Steve.

"Okay," replied Paul.

Steve was walking through the lobby and literally walked right into someone.

"I'm so sorry," Steve looked up

"I'm not, hi Steve," said Lisa.

"Lisa!" Steve exclaimed.

"How's Paul? I was going to ask for an update," asked Lisa.

"He's okay, and he's getting out tomorrow. He's a tough SOB, hard on the outside, mushy in the middle," said Steve.

"Like a piece of fine chocolate," Lisa jokingly added.

"Exactly," Steve answered.

"Well, I better get back to Oliver. It was good RUNNING into you, Steve," said Lisa.

"You too, Lisa. Maybe I'll see you around," answered Steve.

"I hope so. Bye," Lisa ended the conversation.

"Bye," Steve responded.

Lisa walked away.

Way to go, Lin. You messed that up again. Ugh. He called Paul.

"I messed up again. I had a chance to ask Lisa out again. I could find the words," Steve told Paul.

"STEVE!" said Paul.

"She was coming to check on you," Steve continued.

"Really? That girl is a sweetheart. You better not let her get away," responded Paul.

"How do we know she's not after you old man?" asked Steve.

"Well, yeah, but I'll have to let her down easy. You can console her," Paul replied humorously.

Steve got to his car and said, "Thanks a lot. I'll talk to you later. I'm driving."

"Bye," said Paul.

Chapter 4

Paul waited for Jesse, and he was getting a little impatient. He could not wait to get out of the hospital. There was a reason he wanted to get home. Dorie was coming with Scott and the kids.

Paul had to admit that he really missed his family in Minnesota. He missed his youngest son, Ben, too, wherever he was. Ben was a federal agent, right now he was deep undercover, Paul was proud of him and scared out of his mind at the same time.

Paul's grandkids Scotty jr, Noah, and Katie were great kids and had fun hanging with their old Grandpa. Suddenly, Paul perked up at the thought of the kids being there. He loved it when his kids were small, especially Dorie. She always set her brothers straight, and she was the boss. Dorie, the boss, would kick her brothers' butts if they got out of line. Paul laughed to himself.

"That's not the reception I expected. You laughing at me?" Lynne asked.

Paul looked up, his girlfriend Lynne looked beautiful, he loved her so much. "No, honey, I was laughing at the thought of Dorie kicking Ben and Jesse's butts. She was such a tomboy. Where's Jess? I thought he was coming to get me," responded Paul.

Lynne went to him and gave him a kiss.

"You disappointed?" asked Lynne.

"No way, Jose!" replied Paul.

"Jesse had an unscheduled meeting with the mayor about security for the Summer Blast. You know Jess, he loves that stuff," Lynne clarified.

"He always did. Not even sure why he studied to be a lawyer, always knew he'd be in law enforcement, used to follow me around like a shadow," added Paul.

"Come on, let's get you outta here. Gonna have a police escort, sirens and all," Lynne suggested.

"Oh! Fun times!" Paul recalled.

When they got back to the house, everything was quiet. Too quiet. Then Jesse's girlfriend Maddie's Bernese Mountain Dog Tiny barked, then Moose, Maddie's teacup poodle yipped.

"My welcome wagon." Maddie came out and went over to Paul with a big bear hug. "Paul, I'm so glad you're okay!" Paul liked Maddie, like Lynne. She was down to earth, real.

"Thanks, Maddie, you're looking good," Paul said.

Maddie smiled. Maddie quit her job at the local newspaper to concentrate on her writing. The day she quit, Maddie actually wrote half of her first book. It was like floodgates opened for the first time. She was still doing freelance like her old boss and friend Andy, who also left the paper, to go partners and help run Hole in the Wall Hobbies with his friend Ray.

As Paul walked into the house, everyone yelled, 'Surprise'. Steve, Andy, Andy's girlfriend Vee, and the rest of their gang: Joey, Nola, Jimmy, and Jackie. Paul was surprised. Jesse walked out of the kitchen.

"Jess, you trying to give your old man a heart attack?" Paul asked shockingly.

"It was Maddie and Lynne's idea. Truthfully, I think they've been dying for my BBQ ribs." Jesse replied.

Everyone laughed.

"I bet," Paul responded.

"Besides, the Summer Blast is next week. It will give us an opportunity to get some stuff organized, like who's going in the dunk tank!"

Edna walked in the front door with her husband, Marty. "Not me, that's for sure." Edna owned the local coffee shop, Edna's Coffee and Conversation. Nobody made coffee in town. They all went to Edna's.

"Edna, Marty!" Paul was happy to see them.

"I come to see how Paul's doing and I walk into a party. I wasn't invited to. Now we are party crashers, Marty!" She laughed hard, she was invited, her and Paul struck up a wonderful friendship at the shop. "I nominate Lin, maybe getting him in a tiny speedo!"

Everyone was having a good time. Day turned to night, with an excellent BBQ by Jesse. Before you know it, good nights were said. Maddie was staying over.

Paul pulled Jesse to the side and asked, "Jess, is it okay if Lynne stays?"

"You don't need my permission, Dad. Just ask her," replied Jesse.

Paul asked Lynne and she agreed.

It was a wonderful day, and lots got done with the Summer Blast. This is much better than being smushed on the asphalt.

Chapter 5

Paul woke up to the smell of bacon, eggs, pancakes, and coffee. He knew that Lynne and Jesse left for work an hour ago. Maybe Maddie decided to make breakfast. Quickly showering, shaving, and brushing his teeth, Paul made it upstairs from the little basement apartment he made for himself. Entering from opposite sides of the kitchen at the same time, Maddie and Paul saw three little heads at the kitchen table and a beautiful woman leaning against the counter sipping coffee. The three little heads turned to Paul.

"Grandpa!" they all shouted.

Paul looked at Dorie, then back at the kids, as they ran to him. Still very sore, Paul squatted down and scooped the kids into his arms. They knocked Paul on his ass, then Tiny and Moose joined in on the dog pile. Hugs and kisses and dog kisses, Dorie and Maddie laughing huge belly laughs, Paul smiled and laughed himself silly.

"Okay, you guys, let Grandpa up, finish eating, and go watch cartoons for a while." Dorie then turned to Maddie. "Maddie, it's so good to finally see you in person." The two women embraced, and then Dorie turned to her father." Daddy." She fell into her father's arms and didn't want to leave.

"Oh, Dorie, I missed you all so much," Paul said with great warmth in his voice.

"A motorcycle accident at work, why?" Dorie inquired.

"It won't happen again, I promise," Paul swore.

Paul had already decided that was the last time on motorcycles for a while and definitely the last time at work.

"Now, I'm STARVING. Give me everything." The adults laughed and the kids moved a chair between them, for Paul.

Dorie just looked at her kids and laughed. "Guess we have to get our own chairs, Maddie, as long as Grandpa has a seat."

The two ladies laughed. 8-year-old Scotty got two more chairs to the table. "Thank you, Scotty," Maddie said. Scotty ran back to his Grandpa and asked, "Grandpa, can we go for a ride?"

"I can't drive, Scotty, but maybe you can convince one of these beautiful ladies to drive us to the park," replied Paul.

All three kids looked at Dorie and Maddie with pleading eyes. "Please, Mommy," 6-year-old Katie pleaded, and her little shadow, four-year-old Noah, monkey see, monkey do.

"Please, Mommy." Then Paul battered his eyes. "Please, Mommy," the kids cracked up.

Dorie rolled her eyes and said, "Fine." Cheers went up and everyone went to get ready. Everyone, adults, kids, and dogs, loaded Paul's SUV, and Paul gave Dorie instructions on where to go.

"Dad, the park is in the other direction. Those instructions are for the end of Jesse's property," said Dorie.

"Can we just go that way, please? It's kind of a surprise," Paul insisted.

"Oh, sure," answered Dorie.

As they got closer to their destination, Dorie began to understand. "You did not do what I think you did."

"Of course I did!" Paul laughed.

"Mommy, look, horses!" Katie yelled, and of course, Noah chimed in, Horses!" Scotty looked out the window, trying to contain himself.

They got to the stable, and the kids hustled out of the car. Moose and Tiny went into Zoomie mode. Dorie shook her head and threw up her hands. "What the heck?"

"I missed the stables back home. Come on, I'll introduce you to Max, my stable guy. He's good people." The family walked into the stable. Dorie was awestruck .

"Dad, there must be 20 stalls here," said Dorie.

"25 but only 20 horses. Can the kids ride with assistance? Maddie, you ride? I never thought to ask. I'm sorry," Paul answered.

"I was on a horse since I was in diapers. My parents own a few horses, too. They are just not on their property. You have some real beauties here."

Dorie said it was okay for Scotty and Katie to be handled by herself and Maddie. Noah rode with Paul. They took the horses for a small walk, and they talked about how Paul purchased some of Jesse's land to build the stables and possibly build a home back here. Paul did like his son's home setup. He had already looked into different contractors. Jesse thought it was a great idea to ask Maddie to marry him and start a family. He'd need the extra rooms.

Everyone met Max. He was a really sweet guy and pure gentleman. Dorie hadn't missed the fact that there was no wedding band. It was time to head back to the house; the kids were tired and everyone was a little hungry.

Maddie got Dorie on the side.

"Dorie, you have to tell your father," said Maddie.

"How do you know?" Dorie replied.

"I used to be an investigative reporter, remember? There are signs," responded Maddie.

"Yeah, someone should have given me some signs before," said Dorie.

All loaded up, they got home to the smell of the most delicious-smelling burgers ever. Jesse was out back. "Oh, I see. I have to work and you guys get to play with the horses." The kids ran to him, "Uncle Jesse!" chatting away about Grandpa's horses.

Supper went well. The kids were so sleepy they went to bed soon after they ate. They all said good nights and I love you. Maddie went to put coffee on.

Chapter 6

The kids were off to bed. Dorie took a deep breath as Maddie served the coffee.

"Well, I got something to tell you all. It's not so pretty," said Dorie.

Jesse's head jerked up. He never liked Scott, never thought he was good enough for Dorie. Somehow, he knew what she was gonna say but wasn't prepared for the whole story.

Dorie blew out a huge breath of air. "This isn't easy, so I'm just going to spit it out."

Three sets of eyes were glued to Dorie, the tension so strong you could feel it on your skin. "Scott and I are divorced." Paul went over to Dorie, held her in his arms, and asked, "What happened?"

Tears flowed down Dorie's face. She could taste the salt on her lips. She thought, what they must think of me. "We separated 6 months after you left, Daddy," she took a deep breath and then continued, "there was an incident that was not very pleasant."

Dorie searched her mind for the right words, but nothing came to mind to make things better. "Scott came home one night drunk. He started an argument and just picked a fight for no reason at all. When I told him to go sleep it off. He uhhhh, he lunged at me, punched me, the kids came out of their rooms, they saw me, and tried to come to me, but he pushed them… and well. You know what they say about a Mama and her cubs. I went to the safe, got my gun, and told Scott either he left walking out of there or in a body bag. It was his choice."

Paul got up to get his keys.

"Daddy, where are you going?" asked Dorie.

"Minnesota, I'm going kill that bastard with my bare hands," said Paul.

Jesse looked at Maddie and said, "I'm going with you, Dad." Dorie held up her hands. "No one is going anywhere. Going to

Minnesota is useless. Scott is gone. He was criminally charged after I reported him, the chief fired him, he spent a year in jail, he remarried already, and moved to Alaska after giving up custody of the kids."

Paul sat down and put his head in his hands. "This is my fault. I left you if I had been there.." Dorie went over to Paul. "You would have been in jail for murder."

Jesse was just standing there, shaking his head.

"Nobody called us. Dad has a lot of friends, still on the job, and nobody called us. You went through this alone," said Jesse.

"I asked them not to tell you guys, Jesse. Like I said, I did not want you and Dad to wind up in jail over that waste of life," Dorie tried to explain.

Maddie stood up and went over to Dorie. She took her in her arms. They had become fast friends online when Jesse introduced them on FaceTime. They talked every day.

"Are you okay?" Maddie asked Dorie.

"Yes, it all happened over a year ago. Everything is finalized. Some days, I cry, but for the kids, they don't deserve to grow up without a father," explained Dorie. They all nodded in agreement. "I can move back," Paul said.

Dorie gave him a look, her mother's look, when Paul said something crazy. "No, Daddy, you can't. I was actually thinking of keeping the kids here for a while. Figure out what I want to do. Minnesota holds too many bad memories, now."

"Did you close up the house? I can call Butch and close it up and take care of the horses," said Jesse. Dorie smiled, "I already took care of Butch, ummm the other thing is Auntie Mary is going to stay at the house."

Paul let out the biggest laugh ever. Mary was Jessica's sister and still very much part of his family.

"That lady always wanted my house," said Paul.

"So it's okay," added Dorie.

"It's more than okay. I think that's great," answered Paul.

Dorie threw her arms around her father, then motioned for a group hug. Then, four of them embraced.

"I'm still gonna beat the living shit out of Scott if I ever come across him again," said Paul.

"I know, Daddy, I know. I have bail money ready," responded Dorie.

They all laughed at that. Finished up their coffees. Agreed to help Dorie in figuring out what's next. Good nights said they all retired to their rooms.

What a day, Paul thought.

Chapter 7

Maddie, Dorie, and Lynne walked into the Senior center with the three kids in tow. Edna had told them to meet her and Marty there to get stuff done for the Summer Blast party. Edna came out of the little kitchen, followed by Marty and two children.

"Well, hello, I'm glad you made it. I see you brought more helpers to color some papers for the Blast. These are my grandsons, Luke and Colt, and who do we have here?" Edna said with great enthusiasm in her voice.

"Edna, Marty, this is Paul's daughter Dorie and her three kids, Scotty, Katie, and Noah, and I bet they cannot wait to color some pages for the Summer Blast," responded Lynne.

Out of the kitchen came a little girl, then another little girl. Identical twins. "Nana, we need a snack."

"These are my granddaughters, Laney and Lauren," said Edna.

Katie perked up. She thought she was going to be the only girl again. She skipped over to them, and they all giggled. Yep, girls.

Getting the kids settled, then deciding on jobs for the adults. Other volunteers came. Maddie and Jesse's friends Andy and Vee, Jimmy and Jackie, and Joey and Nola were among them. Things were running smoothly. Everyone had a great time. Lemonade and cookies were served. The kitchen was busting at the seams, with all the "chefs" in it. The dishes did look amazing, though. It was also going to be a potluck, which, with record-breaking ticket sales, they are going to need all the food they can get.

Other volunteers were buzzing around, and one of the PTA mothers, Pearl, came up to Dorie and Maddie and said, "Maddie, please tell me you are making both of my favorite dishes for the Summer Blast?"

"Hmmm, what dishes would that be, Pearl," asked Maddie.

"Oh, such the tease, your mouth-watering chicken salad and yummy yummy potato salad," responded Pearl.

"A double yummy? I'll have to make you a bowl for yourself now," said Maddie.

"Oh, then your chicken salad is double yummy too!" Pearl replied humorously.

"Hahaha, okay Pearl, I can take a hint. Oh, where are my manners? Pearl, this is the Sheriff's sister, Dorie," said Maddie.

"Hello Dorie, I can see the resemblance. Mmmmm, is Jesse bringing his ribs?" asked Pearl.

"I certainly hope so," Maddie looked shocked. "I don't think he could remove them before the weekend." Both ladies laughed.

"Maddie!"

"Okay, okay, yes, Jesse is bringing his BBQ ribs. Actually, he will be grilling on-site with his dad, Paul and our friend Andy."

"That's wonderful. How is your dad doing, Dorie?" asked Pearl.

"Well, if you know my father, it would take more than cars whizzing by his head to stop him. He's doing really well. Do you ladies want to know, he told me. He was in the middle of the Highway laughing at the thought of his crime scene silhouette being a circle," Dorie replied.

Maddie looked at her friend. "A circle?"

"Yeah, 'cause he thought he was smushed to the asphalt. That is my crazy father," responded Dorie.

The three of them hooted out laughter so loud that others looked over. Maddie said, "I can picture that."

Pearl went back to her group of friends.

"She was friendly," said Dorie.

Maddie nodded. "Most people in this community are. I mean, a guess, it's in a way, the way we were raised and because most of us lived here our whole lives and instilled that in the children. Your kids are great, by the way, polite and also friendly."

"Noah doesn't remember a lot, but Scotty and Katie went through a tough time with the divorce. I don't think any of us expected that behavior from Scott, except Jesse. He never liked him, never wanted me to marry him," said Dorie.

"Really?" asked Maddie.

"Yep, he was so mad at me, he first refused to be in the wedding party. He only agreed because, well, he's Jesse, and he knows I can kick his butt," continued Dorie.

Maddie and Dorie got back to the task Edna gave them.

By the end of the day, everything was ready for the weekend. The Summer Blast this year will be exceptional, bigger, better, and loads of fun.

Dorie's eyes drifted to Maddie's left. There was Max, the guy in charge of Paul's stable. Max was handsome in a rugged cowboy sort of way. Maddie noticed the way Dorie was looking and turned to see Max, her head turning back to Dorie, mouth opened, then back to Max, who caught them looking and gave a sheepish wave. Maddie and Dorie waved back, and Maddie let her breathe go.

"You like Max!" said Maddie.

"No, no, Maddie, I don't even know Max," answered Dorie.

"Uh-huh," Maddie responded.

The kids came over and they literally looked exhausted. It was late and they would need to eat.

Dorie picked up Noah. Maddie took Scott and Katie's hands. "Okay, gang, let's call it a day."

Chapter 8

Andy and Jesse were working on the staging and booths. There were a handful of volunteers, but most of the major stuff was done. Paul had the grandkids, and they were just hanging out, watching.

Paul had been doing a lot of thinking about the future and as much as he loved being a cop, he missed being around his grandkids. He kept thinking maybe Dorie and the kids could stay in Poland, Maine. He hasn't brought it up with Dorie, but gosh, it sounded darn good.

Paul wasn't around much for his kids, making money to pay the bills. He did a lot of overtime. By the time Paul blinked his eyes, Ben had already graduated from the academy. I haven't even seen Benny in two years, Paul thought to himself. The last time Paul heard from Benny, he was in Colombia. It was scary knowing his little boy was running with drug lords. Ben's answer was, "Someone has to stop them, Dad."

"What are you daydreaming about, old man," a voice appeared.

Paul looked up to see Steve Lin.

"Hey! You made it. These are my grandkids: Scotty, Katie, and Noah. Kids, this is Steve, Officer Lin, he's a really good friend of mine. Steve is also the guy I plan to dunk at the Summer Blast," said Paul.

The kids cheered, and Steve laughed.

"You know, you have the hit the bullseye, Wiseman," responded Steve.

"Oh Lin, I have been practicing, and I'm good!" replied Paul. Andy and Jesse came over with Jimmy and Joey. Jesse wound up for an imaginary pitch.

"Oh yeah, kaplunk in the dunk."

Jimmy started singing, "Splish Splash, I was taking a bath at the Summer Blast!"

Steve shook his head. "I need to find Edna. I think I'm going to be sick this weekend."

Everyone got a good laugh.

The kids were getting tired, and Noah wanted Paul to carry him. "Alright, I guess we are good to go."

Back at Jesse's, the ladies were getting the food together. Potato salad, macaroni salad, finger sandwiches made with chicken salad, egg salad, ham and cheese, turkey and cheese, and

Mini Italian 'subs. Everything was made in triple batches.

Jesse had loads and loads of marinated ribs and, of course, all the dishes people would be bringing. Jimmy's chef at his restaurant was making desserts, cookies and cakes, and mini pastries. Enough to feed an army.

Again, everything was coming together, and the Blast was just like a big family reunion but of the people who make up this wonderful community.

"I don't know about anyone else, but all this food is making me hungry. I have coffee and muffins. Shall we?"

They all chimed in, "We shall!"

The Summer Blast was in less than two days. Everyone was so excited, you could feel it in the air.

Chapter 9

The next morning, Maddie was on the phone. The toy prizes for the races and the Summer Blast Kiddie games had not come yet. It was a big disappointment.

"How can you sit there and tell me to calm down, that everything will be fine? You expect me to be happy. Are you telling me I'll get them by Monday? I need them today. Please cancel that order. No, I don't care that it shipped. I am refusing it and stopping payment. You have disappointed a lot of children. I don't really care. Pay for it yourself. Good day." Furious, Maddie slammed down her phone on the counter.

"Whoa, Tempers high, check. What's up, Maddie?"

"The toy prizes, they won't get here till Monday. I don't have any clue what to do," replied Maddie.

"You are kidding, right? DORIE!"

"Dad, tone it down to a shout. What's wrong?"

"Maddie needs toys, and she doesn't know what to do," said Paul.

DORIE looked from her father to Maddie. "Really?" Maddie shrugged.

"Kids, let's go, we are going to..." Paul continued.

She looked at her father.

"Wally World!!!" added Paul.

Maddie laughed, catching on.

Everyone loaded up in Paul's SUV again, the dogs staying home this time. "You know what's crazy? I would have never thought of this on my own," Maddie said.

Dorie shook her head. "It's because you haven't any kids yet. When you have kids, you always always need something. You know what I mean?"

"I actually do. My life is full of schedules and lists, memos, and little Post-it notes. I hardly have issues like these. Thank you both," said Maddie.

Paul laughed. "Don't thank us yet. I'm guessing you have never been shopping with Jesse besides the market."

"You mean, the mall or Walmart? Not that I remember," replied Maddie.

"Kids! She never shopped with a Wiseman!" said Paul.

"WISEMAN RULE!" Then they giggled

When Scott gave up parental rights, Dorie changed hers and the kids' names back to Wiseman.

Maddie never laughed so hard.

"Wally World, watch out. Here comes the Wiseman family!"

So when they got to Walmart, everyone was super excited, the kids realizing that these toys were for the Summer Blast, that the online store messed up the order and that there would be lots of kids winning games with no prizes.

"That stinks," Scotty said.

Paul ruffled his hair, "That's right, that's why we are going to help."

They went for the smaller prizes first. Timeless favorites like punching balls, paddles with a super ball on end, toy dinosaurs, some little beany dolls, and stuffed toys. Onto racing prizes Mini Basketballs, soccer balls, footballs, skip it, hula hoops, bigger dolls with bottles, transformers, and lastly, the decorations for bikes and carriages. Two $25 gift cards to Walmart and two of the newest handheld games.

Paul told the kids to go pick something for themselves to help. Paul didn't even blink an eye at the total; he just handed the clerk his credit card.

Maddie shook her head, "Paul, I can't let you do that. I'm going to pay you back with the funds."

"No, Maddie, just save it for Labor Day or Halloween. Boooooo," replied Paul.

Maddie gave Paul a quick hug. Of course, they sent Noah over to Paul.

"Grandpa?" said Noah.

"Oh, my littlest Noah, do you need something?" asked Paul.

"Can we get ice cream?" added Noah.

"Ice cream? Did Scotty and Katie make you come over?" Paul asked.

Noah nodded with great enthusiasm, and Paul laughed. "Yes, we can get ice cream."

Maddie and Dorie clapped! "Next stop, ICE CREAM!"

After ice cream, they dropped all the stuff at the Senior Center, where other volunteers would transport it in the morning.

Chapter 10

Everyone agreed to meet at Jesse's the morning of the Summer Blast to haul all the food, and boy, did they have food. Jimmy had Dino bring the desserts straight to the park.

Dino was so proud of himself, making all kinds of Fourth of July-themed pastries. Flag cookies, red, white, and blue half-moons.

Flag cakes with whipped cream, strawberries, blueberries, and of course…Apple pies. Dino also made some sausage, peppers, and onion trays.

Everyone wanted everyone else to have the best time. That's what these outings were about - Community, Togetherness, Support.

Team Wiseman all got to the park at 9 a.m., and the kid races were starting at that time. All three kids were doing all the activities they could. Lynne brought her nephew David, who was 10. Both David's parents worked two jobs, and he was mostly with Lynne when she wasn't working.

He fit right in with Dorie's kids and he had brought his decorated bike, hoping to win one of the big prizes.

Edna came up to the group; she and Marty were dressed as Uncle Sam and Betsy Ross. "I want to thank you all for your hard work and dedication. Paul, the prizes are wonderful. The food everyone brought is enough food to feed an army."

Steve Lin, who told Paul he'd meet them at the park, showed up in a 1920s bathing suit. Paul nearly choked on his drink, "You still going in the dunk, Steve."

"Come on, Paul, you can't hit the side of a barn with those chicken wings," replied Steve.

"Maybe not, but she can, champion all-state softball pitcher. You remember Lisa and Oliver, don't you, Steve?" asked Paul.

Paul introduced the two medics to his family, then said to Lisa. "Doesn't Steve look cute in his bath suit? He's ready to get dunked." Lisa laughed.

"I'm going in the tank. See Wiseman, I told you, I knew you were mean from day one." Steve waved and went to the tank.

Everyone had a wonderful time, filling their bellies and checking out the kids playing games and racing. Each kid won a different game. Scotty won his age race, Katie and Noah got second place in their races, and David won the bike decorating contest.

Steven got dunked about 70 times. Lisa came up to the dunk tank with Oliver. Steve was upset that the two medics seemed to be together like on a date. Lisa said to Steve. "Do I get a prize if I dunk you?"

"Like what?" asked Steve.

"You take me to movies and dinner," replied Lisa.

"What do I get if you miss?" asked Steve.

"I'll let you take me to dinner and a movie," Lisa responded and Steve laughed.

"Won't your boyfriend mind?" Steve asked Lisa.

"My boyfriend? Oliver? Oh my God, that is too funny," replied Lisa and got behind the line and wound up her pitch. Swish, bullseye, in the tank went Steve. Lisa walked up to the tank.

"I like Chinese and chick flicks…oh and Steve, Oliver is gay," Lis told Steve.

Steve was relieved from the dunk tank. Lisa and Oliver were waiting for him.

"Mmmmm, I can't wait for that delicious meal. I'll be eating after that tear-jerker movie." Oliver laughed at Lisa.

"Okay, okay, pick on the loser. Did you guys eat yet? There's a lot of good arms around here. I was in the dunk about eighty times."

"No, I made Oliver wait till you were done. He's starving."

"Well, let's go, man, food is awaiting!"

Making their way over to Paul, Steve asked Lisa if she'd go out with him on a real date, not the bet.

"Of course, I think your friend Paul had given up hope on you," replied Lisa. Oliver piped in, "Me too. You kept missing your target, Steve.

Paul saw Lisa and Oliver with Lin. He gave Steve a big applause, to which Steve gave a huge bow.

"It's about time, Lin. I was going to paint a bullseye on Lisa."

Somebody pushed Paul forward.

"Sorry about that."

Paul didn't even look. "No problem."

Then the guy said in a loud voice. "This food is lame, not one cup of Yankee Doodle pudding. Fourth of July and no Yankee Doodle Pudding."

Paul smiled, remembering when the kids were small, Jessica always had Yankee Doodle cupcakes. They were Benny's favorite. The guy got close to Paul again, nudging him. Jesse came over. "All right, Pal, back it up."

"Sorry, sorry, I was just trying to get close to a barrel in case those god-awful ribs make me puke, really dry, and the sauce tastes like metal."

"What? You got some nerve," said Jesse.

Paul grabbed the guy and turned to face him. The younger man smiled at him. "Hi, dad!"

Paul blinked.

"Benny?" His son was all grown up. He leaned down, his face was chiseled, and he looked wonderful. Paul fell into tears, and he grabbed his son.

Jesse said, "I should have known when you put down my ribs."

"Oh no, those really were awful, bro." The brothers hugged and Paul hugged them.

Dorie had come back from getting the kids some ice cream, seeing the group hug. "Hey! What's going on?"

"Hey, Sticks." Ben's nickname for his once long-legged sister. Dorie let out a little joy. "Benny!"

"Can you image no Yankee Doodle pudding?" laughed Benny.

"I will make some at home," Dorie replied.

Everyone gathered around, from Paul's group to be introduced to Benny. The kids finally got close enough, and Scotty saw who it was.

"Uncle Benny!" Of course, the other two yelled too, though they had been much younger to remember. The rest of the event was going well and everyone was happy.

There was a brief moment when Noah disappeared, and everyone started freaking out. They spread out, the area of the party was not that big, and the park was fenced in. It had been 20 minutes before they located him, the longest 20 minutes in time for Dorie. The family was at first worried that someone had grabbed him, but Dorie had said Noah has a bad habit of walking away. Noah had to decide adults were boring and went to the little petting zoo. Dorie scooped him up.

"Oh Noah, you give your mama a little heart attack."

Of course, Noah, not understanding, just smiled and pointed to the animals, "Horses!"

Everyone laughed and took a relieving breath.

Chapter 11

Andy made his way over to the dunk tank. He knew who Steve's relief was. The co-owner of Hole in the Wall Hobbies and Andy's partner and friend, Ray.

Ray and his son Frankie got up every morning before work to swim in their underground pool. Andy thought Ray would do a great job in the dunk tank. He loved teasing customers at the shop. Sure enough, Ray was heckling a couple of teenagers.

"I've seen better wings on a bird."

Thud, Miss.

"Your mama better take you home, Sonny. It's past your bedtime."

Thud. Miss.

"Look at that big kid, Whadda say, you look outta shape."

Andy laughed, paid for two balls, went to the line, and did a little exaggerated wind-up.

Thud. Miss.

"Wow! We should not have taken your money, you st..."

Bong. Dunk.

Andy walked up to the tank. "Fake out!"

"Sure, sure," Ray got back on the board.

One old lady came up behind Andy and whacked him with her purse. "Hoodlum! Are you okay, Ray?" Other old ladies came up to check on Ray.

"Unbelievable, Ray, you've got cheerleaders," said Andy.

"Well, young Andy, when you got it, you got it. I got it!" replied Ray.

Andy went back to his group. He was still laughing, his girlfriend Vee knew he was causing havoc.

"What did you do?" Andy puffed up proudly. "I dunked Ray and got whacked with a purse by a little old lady protecting him." Vee laughed. Andy took her in his arms and kissed her.

Steve just wanted a few minutes with Lisa and thought he saw the perfect moment. Benny and Oliver were in a conversation. Oliver was telling Benny how he was going to Med school while EMTing.

"Hey there." Steve slipped beside Lisa.

"Hey, yourself," replied Lisa.

"Lisa, I'm glad we found each other here. I would have never thought you guys would be at the Summer Blast," continued Steve.

"Steve, Paul invited us while he was in the ambulance." Steve laughed. "Of course, He did as he told me that I better not let you get away."

"I'm glad your friend is watching out for you. I like you Steve, you are sweet," said Lisa.

"I like you, too. Come on, let's get back to the others," replied Steve.

Oliver laughed so much that he had tears. I never met anyone like Benny, he thought to himself.

"Can I ask you something personal?" asked Oliver.

"Sure, Oliver, what is it?" said Benny.

"Are you, umm, do you, what I mean is.." Oliver tried to continue. Benny let out a low, sexy chuckle.

"I'm unattached, Oliver. Would you like to go to dinner this week? I'd love to get to know you better," Benny asked Oliver.

"Yes, Yes, I'd really like to. I have the next three days off," Oliver answered in excitement.

"Well, then let's make a day of it tomorrow. Come by Jesse's whenever time in the morning," replied Benny.

They walked back toward the group. Both men looked extremely happy. It was time for the fireworks, and it was such a beautiful display on a clear night.

The day was coming to a close, and it was a wonderful event. Edna and Marty came over. "We just want to thank everyone. Great job. Everything was wonderful."

Chapter 12

When Paul and the family got back to the house, they found Max on their front steps. Paul noticed he was a little roughed up, like in a scuffle with someone. "Max? What's going on? Are you okay?"

Now, everyone was standing around Max.

"I'm fine. I was locking up, and someone hit me from behind… Paul, they took some of the younger horses and Ginger," replied Max.

Ginger was Paul's horse. She had come with him from Minnesota, she was a prize-winning racehorse and all her babies were 'sure' things. Paul only bred Ginger because of her beauty and manner.

Dorie went to look at Max's eye. It looked awful.

"Max, you need to have that looked at. Your eye is all red. You might have a concussion," Dorie instructed Max.

Jesse and Lynne agreed that Max should have it checked. Benny volunteered to stay with the kids while Dorie and Maddie took Max.

Paul, Jesse, and Lynne headed to the stables. Paul was beside himself, thinking Ginger was already older. Why would anybody want her except him? He loved her.

It was after 11 p.m. when they got to the stables. All the horses reared up. They knew something was wrong.

Jesse called the sheriff's department to report the crime.

Wally told him that they were the second call tonight about stolen horses. Terrific. Jesse told Wally to grab a couple of guys and come over for a statement.

"On my way, Sheriff," said Wally.

The crooks weren't too smart. They left behind a lot of evidence. One of them left a ball cap behind, plus a shoe print. Paul had Max install a security camera last month. The whole crime was caught, but it was hard to see the thief.

"We'll get them back, dad."

Paul just nodded. Up till a few weeks ago, life was so uneventful he gave out a huge sigh. The three of them headed back to the house. Jesse got Benny up to date. Now, all they could do was wait. Paul's horses were all tattooed on their underside, so selling them would be impossible. I hope they just release them when they notice.

Maddie and Dorie came back with Max. "The doctor said he's just shaken up, but I'd feel better if he stayed so we could watch him."

Jesse agreed with Dorie. Jesse put Max in a guest room, which was now entirely full. Last year, it was just me and Dad. Now I have a full house. Not that I'm complaining, Jesse thought to himself; this is where he wanted family, right here with me. Soon enough, I'll ask Maddie if she wants to get married to me and my crazy family. Jesse knew Dorie wasn't going back, and there was nothing left for her in Minnesota.

"Jesse, you don't have to do this. I'll be fine at home, and I'll just take it easy," said Max.

"Max, what's the problem? Just kick back here and let the ladies take care of you. They love fawning over you. Must be your Ughhhly mug," Jesse replied. Max laughed. Max and Jesse were friends for a long time and when Paul asked him to manage Paul's stable, he jumped at it.

Dorie came into the guest room. Max and Jesse stopped talking and looked at her, then at each other, and broke out laughing.

Dorie turned and walked out of the guest room. "Okay."

Jesse laughed so hard he had tears.

"Boy, Max, you are in trouble!" said Jesse.

"Thanks a lot," Max responded humorously.

Tiny and Moose decided that Max did not need the whole king-size bed and curled up with him. "Looks like you made some new friends, cute." Max chuckled.

Chapter 13

Paul was inconsolable; he loved Ginger, and those colts were his babies. His thoughts, of late, were that he was going to retire at the end of the year, have the house built, ask Lynne to marry him, and just ride Ginger every day.

Paul knew running out and checking every stable in the area was fruitless. Ginger and the colts were probably gone, especially where there were other stolen horses, not as valuable, but to the owner, they were probably priceless. A good lead was the best Paul could hope for.

Lynne came into the parlor, where Paul was sitting, watching out the window. Sitting on the arm of the oversized chair Paul was on, Lynne massaged the back of his neck. "Honey, come to bed. There's nothing we can do at this hour."

"Aww Lynne, all I keep thinking is if they are hurting her. These thieves take animals to breed. Ginger is done; she doesn't have the strength to go through another pregnancy," replied Paul.

"I know, Paul, the guys are working hard on this and they are talking to everyone who has anything to do with both stables," said Lynne.

"Yeah, but you know me, patience is not my strong point," answered Paul.

Lynne laughed and said, "We just need to keep the faith."

Paul took a deep breath, "What would I do without you?"

"I just don't know, really," Lynne responded.

The next day, Benny was up early. He thought about his dad most of the night and if truth be told, he felt his pain. Remembering when Paul brought Ginger home to Minnesota, his dad was lit up like a Christmas tree, so proud like Ginger was his newborn child.

Something didn't sit right with Benny. His gut told him there were answers at the other stable, maybe clues, that were missed.

Benny decided he needed to get in there, maybe talk up the help. It was even a bigger stable than Dad's. The difference was that the horses taken from the other stable were not what you would call winning horses. Of course, maybe the thief or thieves didn't know the difference. I'm going find out, Benny thought to himself.

Jesse was sitting at his desk when George Ames came in. George was the other horse owner that was robbed. Jesse couldn't help but wonder why George would be here. Jesse's deputies gathered all the evidence they could and took everyone's statements.

"George?" said Jesse.

"Jesse (silence followed), any word?" questioned George.

"Come on, George, really, you know, I'd call you. What's really bothering you," asked Jesse.

"I'm just afraid that everyone would be looking for your father's horses and mine.." George tried to continue, but Jesse cut him off, saying, "I don't work that way, George. I'm kinda offended by that."

"I'm sorry, Jesse, I'm just so upset," George apologized.

"George, you didn't answer the deputies when they asked if that was all your employees. Was anyone fired recently, anyone working off the books?" Jesse asked.

"Two punks were fired, but I heard they caught the B&M down to Boston, that's it," replied George.

"You heard?" Jesse responded.

"Couple of the stable boys told me," George answered.

"Okay, well George, I'm going to tell you, I am not putting any less effort into finding your horses than my Dad's. I, actually, got more helpful information off of him about your horses than you and your workers combined," Jesse informed George.

"Thanks Jesse, and I'm sorry. Tell your dad I'm thinking of him. Happy Fourth of July," said George.

"You bet. You too," replied Jesse.

Chapter 14

The doorbell rang and three children made a mad dash with two barking dogs on their heels.

"Who is it?" Scotty asked.

"Oliver." The three looked at each other.

"Do we know an Oliver?" Katie said.

"We don't know you."

"I'm here for your uncle Benny," said Oliver.

Benny came in and opened the door. "Good job, guys, this is Oliver, he's my friend." The kids said hello. Lynne and Dorie came into the front room. Benny said to them, "You two remember Oliver? We are going to dinner. I'll be home later."

"Well, have a great time," Dorie said.

"Thank you. Nice seeing you ladies again." Oliver shook the ladies' hands. The guys left in Oliver's car just as Paul and Max came up from the stables. Paul gave a quick wave.

Paul and Max went inside, and Max said he was going to lie down a little bit. Paul turned to the ladies. "Where are Benny and Oliver off to?" Lynne and Dorie looked at each other, and Dorie said. "They went out to dinner, Dad." Paul's response was not what they expected. He said, "Well, it's about time he met someone." Both women laughed. "Dad, you knew? Benny told you?"

"Told me? Dorie, I've known your brother was gay for a long time. No, he never told me or your mother. We just knew. He's a good man, good head on his shoulders, who he wants to be involved with is his business, not mine," explained Paul.

Lynne went over and gave him a quick peck on the cheek. "Good for you. That is being a supportive father." Paul went to get washed up.

Maddie came out of her "writing room," which Jesse had made her a little home office. Not wanting to put her old landlords out, she was waiting for Stan and Dot to find a new tenant before she officially moved in with Jesse.

"I'm going to put something on for supper. Did I miss anything while I was writing?" asked Maddie.

Lynne and Dorie told her about Benny and how Paul responded when they told him. "Well, in this day and age, people should be more accepting. They are happy, so be happy for them," said Maddie.

"Amen to that," replied Dorie.

Benny and Oliver got to the restaurant. It was on the coast, a very nice place with an outdoor balcony. They hadn't had a reservation but got lucky and the waitress gave them one of the seatings on the balcony.

They talked and ate and talked some more. The evening flew by.

"Oliver, by this time on my dates, I'm asked about being a Federal Agent, and that's the only topic anybody ever talks to me about. You hadn't even mentioned it, and it's refreshing," said Benny.

"To be honest, it scares me a little, but right now, we are just out having a good time, right? We don't know what the future holds, but I can tell you. I had the most wonderful evening. It's been a while since I've been out with a charming man who listens and cares about what I'm saying," Oliver replied.

Benny reached across the table and held Oliver's hand. "Can I see you again?"

"You better," Oliver responded.

Jesse came home as the ladies were putting the food on the dining room table. He went over and gave Maddie a kiss, and Tiny and Moose waited for their kisses; everyone laughed. Paul and Max came into the dining room. Then Jesse said. "Where's Benny?" A quick glance went around the table. "Okay, what's going on?"

Paul told Jesse about Benny and Oliver.

"Benny's gay? I don't understand," Jesse was surprised.

"Jess!!" Paul tried to lower his voice.

"Well, I'm sorry, I'm a little slow to accept these things, but he's my brother and this is the first time I'm hearing it," Jesse responded.

"Honey," Maddie started to say. "It's nobody's business who he sees."

Jesse shook his head. "I'm going out to the stable."

"Jesse, it's been gone over with a fine tooth comb. The only way to get the horses back is if we get lucky," Paul added.

"George Ames came by today, accusing me of looking harder for your horses," Jesse told Paul.

"That doesn't sound like George. Weird," said Paul.

"So I reviewed both of your statements and there are just some things that are just not adding up. None of them said anything about the two stable boys that George let go. That could be something, or it could be nothing but when you leave things out. It doesn't help," Jesse continued.

Maddie looked at Jesse, "Please come eat. Being upset isn't going to change anything."

"Wonderful meal, ladies," Max said, looking better since he came home.

Maddie said, "Hope you left room for Dorie's wonderful dessert. Apple pie!"

"Oh boy! My favorite!" Max fit right in.

The front door opened, and Benny walked in with Oliver. Benny's smile said it all. He was happy. "Is that Dorie's apple pie?"

Jesse went over and shook Oliver's hand.

"I hope you and Benny left some room for some big pieces of pie!" Dorie said.

"Oh yeah!" Oliver replied.

Chapter 15

Joey Micheals was sitting in a small cafe, sipping coffee. Joey is Maddie's childhood best friend. Joey, Maddie, and Jimmy are the three musketeers. Joey is dating Nola, who is Maddie's best friend. Joey was sitting talking on the phone with Nola when two ranch hands came in. They were whispering among themselves, but Joey heard the words horses and sick. Telling Nola he had to call her back, Joey pretended to check his phone while listening to the conversation.

"We need to get rid of that old horse. She's useless. She can't be bred in that condition."

"What do you suppose we do? Shoot her?"

"No, stupid! Just let her go."

Joey called Jesse. "Jess, get to the Friendly cafe now. Hurry."

Joey hung up and saw that the men were getting their coffees to go. How can I stall? He thought to himself. Getting up to throw away his coffee, Joey pretended to trip and spill his coffee on the men.

The men quickly brushed off Joey, trying to help them. They hadn't seen the man exiting the cafe. The men left the cafe and pulled away as Jesse pulled up to a waving Joey.

"Jess, follow that blue truck. They were in there, talking about horses. I think they were talking about Ginger and the Colts." Joey told him as he got in the car.

"What?" Jesse got on his radio and called his deputies for backup.

"They kept saying horses and sick and letting her go," replied Joey.

Jesse called his father, and he told Paul his location and the way he was heading. The men must have realized the sheriff was following them. They lost Jesse after a few twists.

None of the deputies saw anyone and Jesse was pissed with himself. Then, Jesse's phone rang.

"Jess." It was Benny. He told Jesse to follow the road he was on; he'll come to a clearing with what looks like a farmhouse, but it's a front for a barn.

Jesse pumped the gas and took off. Telling Joey how he thinks Benny has them. Jesse thought to himself and laughed, "Only Benny." Jesse had his deputies surround the property, and Paul pulled his truck next to Jesse's. Max was in the car with Paul.

Paul, Jesse, and Lynne, who showed up with the deputies, huddled together. Paul kept his voice low.

"What do we do?" Jesse looked at his father. Lynne answered first.

"Well, we can't just storm in because we don't know if the horses are in there. This place isn't even supposed to be occupied. I don't want them to be watching us and start shooting."

"Yeah."

Then gunshots. Jesse grabbed his rifle out of his car, then looked up and saw Benny coming out from the side of the farmhouse.

"Don't you dare shoot me, Jesse." Big Goofy Benny grin on his face. He was pulling two men cuffed to each other and one hopping. "Might want to call a medic."

Lynne and Paul went and cuffed the men separately and handed them off to the deputies.

"Benny?" Paul looked at his son.

"I was in the coffee shop, I was following them, I just had this feeling, 'cause they were lurking around George's place...I saw Joey spill the coffee on them. Nice stall, Joe. I went out to my car and followed them. When they got to the barn and opened the door, I saw Ginger. I identified myself, hopped over there, and pulled his gun. I shot him in the foot." Benny justified everything.

Everyone thought that was hilarious.

"All the horses are in the barn. I called George. He's on his way."

"Dad, go see Ginger, she's very anxious," said Jesse. Paul and Lynne went off to check on Ginger and the kiddies.

Jesse patted Benny's shoulder. "You did good, and I'm so glad you're here."

"Yeah, me too, Jesse. I'm sorry I didn't tell you." Jesse knew Benny was talking about being gay.

"What? No, I'm sure that was hard for you. I guess I got a little upset cause I thought maybe you thought you couldn't tell me. I just want you to know you are my brother and I love you. Nothing you can do will ever change that. Unless you break the law, I'll haul your ass to jail." They both laughed, big belly laughs.

"Come on. I heard the sirens. Maybe it's a lover boy." Benny punched his brother. "Shaddup!"

The medics weren't Oliver and Lisa. Benny had to admit he was a little disappointed, but it wasn't like he shot that punk for that reason. Right?

Back at Jesse's place, George came by. He wanted to thank everyone and brought a huge tray of his wife's chicken cutlets with a side of tomato sauce and several loaves of homemade French bread.

Benny was in heaven. There was a knock at the door. Paul yelled for Benny to get to the door. "Boy, getting his horses back wasn't enough," Benny said sarcastically. When the door swung open, there was Oliver, carrying yet another tray.

"I heard dessert was needed."Oliver put the tray on the table and pulled back the lid. Benny's eyes lit up.

"Yankee Doodle pudding!!!" All the kids came running. Benny grabbed two puddings.

"How did you know?" Benny asked Oliver.

"Actually, it was Lynne's idea. She made them, but they weren't for rescuing the horses. She invited me for dinner before everything happened today," replied Oliver.

Benny went over and gave Lynne a hug and a peck on the cheek. "Thank you."

Chapter 16

Things started to get back to normalcy. Paul needed to get back to work, but could he? The more he thought about it, the more he was certain that he really wanted to put on his badge again. He called up Steve and asked if he would want to come over for a while to have a beer.

"Give me 20 minutes, I'll be there." Something is up, Steve thought to himself. Paul didn't sound like himself.

Twenty minutes later, Steve pulled into the Wiseman driveway. Paul was at the doorway, holding four beers. He walked over, sat in one of the old rockers on the porch, and motioned Steve to the other. Passing Steve two beers, Paul said, "I am going to run something by you. Tell me what you think."

"I'll tell you, Paul, you're making me nervous," said Steve.

"I think I want to retire for good now." It caught Steve off guard, and he didn't know what to say.

"I know this is out of the blue, Steve, but it's real, and I think it's time," Paul continued.

"Is this because of the accident?" asked Steve.

"No, No. I think it's just I'm in a different place now than when I left Missouri. I have Lynne, and Dorie might stay here with the kids. I could watch them when she gets a job. You know, I can keep busy now," replied Paul.

Steve wanted to be positive, but he wasn't sure if those were good enough reasons for Paul to retire.

"You're against it, aren't you?" asked Paul.

"I dunno, Paul. I guess I don't understand it," replied Steve.

"OK, I don't feel the same rush to get up and get to work anymore. I don't need to be a cop anymore to complete my life. I guess I can't explain it. I want to be around to see my grandkids grow up, and this job is wearing me down," Paul told Steve.

"Okay," Steve replied.

"Okay?" asked Paul.

"Yeah, I mean, you accomplished everything there was to give in Minnesota. You came here and gave it a couple more years. I guess you're ready now. How are you going to tell the captain?" asked Steve.

"He's the least of my problems. Wait till I tell my family. They will be stuck with me 24 hours a day," said Paul.

"Aw hell, they'll love it! They will find a million things for you to do," replied Steve.

Paul and Steve sat back and finished their beers. They talked about Steve's new girlfriend, Lisa, and Benny and Oliver. Paul told Steve how he planned on proposing to Lynne and building the house twice as large. A separate apartment for Dorie and the kids and maybe a guest suite.

"Sounds great, Paul," Steve said.

" Thanks, Man," Paul replied.

After Steve left, Paul took Ginger out for a ride, she was still really anxious and Paul hoped their rides would help her. The rides helped Paul clear his head and think about how to tell the family.

Paul waited for everyone to sit down to eat supper. He made lasagna with jumbo meatballs.

In the middle of the meal, the conversation turned to Paul being excited about going back to work. Paul was quiet.

"Dad?" Jesse looked at his father. Dorie did, too. "Daddy, what's wrong?"

Paul shook his head, "Nothing, nothing's wrong. I just thought if I didn't go back to work, you all would have me doing all the cooking and cleaning."

Jesse and Dorie looked at each other. Paul laughed. "Don't look so shocked."

"Dad, are you serious? " Jesse was happy for his father. It must have been the hardest decision of his life.

"Dead serious, but I have one more thing to do," Paul responded.

Everyone looked at him. Paul got up, took Lynne's hand, and walked her over to the small sofa in the dining room.

"Lynne, from the day I met you, you have completed my life." Paul got down on one knee and took out a small jewelry box. Everyone became silent.

"Will you make me the happiest man in the world and be my wife?" He opened the box, and the ring was beautiful," Paul continued.

Lynne was crying. "Yes," she whispered.

"What we didn't hear you?" Paul teased her.

"YES, I'll marry you, Paul Wiseman. I love you," Lynne said overexcitedly.

"I love you, too," Paul replied.

Everyone ran in to hug the happy couple.

Chapter 17

Jesse got a couple of beers and a glass of wine for Maddie as they headed out back to the fire pit. The dogs went to find some rabbits to chase in the dark while Jesse and Maddie snuggled close together.

"What a day! Your dad is really full of surprises," said Maddie.

"I know, Mads, but I'm kind of upset with him," replied Jesse.

"Because he's retiring?" asked Maddie.

Jesse stood up. "No, 'cause he stole our spotlight."

"Jesse, what are you talking about?" Maddie asked shockingly. Jesse kneeled on one knee before Maddie. She gasped, "Mads, I'm not great with words like my father, but I know I do love you, and I want to spend the rest of my life making you happy. Maddie Stevens, will you be my wife."

With more tears, Maddie was emotionally drained. "Of course I will. I love you too."

They kissed, Jesse sat down, and they just sat there, holding each other tight. What a night.

Chapter 18

Benny sat at the dining room table with a bowl of cereal. He had been up most of the night.

He was kind of wired about getting Ginger back if he had to admit he loved the old girl as much as his father. It was Ginger that Benny finally agreed to take riding lessons because she was so gentle.

Looking around the kitchen, Benny realized how much he really missed being in a real home, not a little four-wall apartment. He certainly could afford better, but what was the point? I'm by myself, and being an undercover agent didn't feel right anymore. If Benny was truthful with himself, being a federal agent wasn't all it cracked up to be anymore. He was proud of his dad for knowing when to walk away. How would I feel about walking away? Benny thought to himself. It's not like he had any real friends at the agency because he wasn't around that much.

Jesse came in and grabbed a bowl. "Thinking again, are we little brother?"

"Yeah, Jess, I do that every once in a while," Benny replied.

"Anything you need my superior advice on?" asked Jesse.

"Maybe, what would I be if I wasn't an agent anymore?" questioned Benny.

"You too?"

Benny nodded.

"I'll tell you, Benny, I thought I'd be old and gray before I heard those words from you. You my brother, like me, were smart because we got that college education before signing on. Most just go straight to the academy like Dad. To your question, anything you want to be."

Benny looked at Jesse dead seriously.

"I want to be a ballerina," said Benny.

Jesse almost choked, laughing at his cereal. "I bet you do, brother. I bet you do."

You know Jesse, you look different, like ohohoh you got a secret," Benny continued.

"How do you do that?" asked Jesse.

"I'm the youngest. I always need ammunition against you and Dorie. Spill," said Benny.

"Okay, Maddie didn't want rain on Dad's parade, so we were going to keep quiet this week. I asked Maddie to marry me," Jesse told Benny.

A gasp came from behind Jesse, and there was Dorie. "Oh my Gosh, and you were going to tell HIM, and not me!"

"A little dramatic, Dor?" Benny said.

She ran and hugged Jesse from behind. "I like her," Dorie said, smiling.

Jesse laughed. " I like her too."

Dorie grabbed a bowl and the three siblings munched and whispered through breakfast.

Maddie heard Jesse leave and others shuffling around the house. It was almost 7 a.m., pretty early for most but not for Nola. She would be heading to the gym to, as she would say, 'get my groove' on.

Maddie dialed, and the phone rang once.

"Where is Maddie and why do you have her phone?" Nola asked.

Maddie laughed. "It's me silly. Can you keep a secret?"

"Well, it must be a good one to have you up before 8," said Nola.

"It is," Maddie responded.

"You finished your book," asked Nola.

"I wish. Jesse asked me to marry him," Maddie told Nola.
There was a thud.

"Nola, did you just fall off the treadmill," Maddie was curious.

"No, no.. yes, ouch," Nola responded.

Maddie tried not to laugh but couldn't help it, and then Nola laughed too.

"You okay?" asked Maddie.

"I'll live, wow, marriage," said Nola.

"I know, I thought maybe it's too soon, what do you think?" Maddie continued.

"Are you kidding, Mads? I never saw two people more comfortable and in love as you two are with each other. Besides, you don't have to get married next week. Do you?" Nola responded.

"Nola! No, we do not," said Maddie.

"Whew!" Nola replied.

After breakfast, Dorie took the kids and got in the car to go down to the stable. Paul wanted to go, too.

"Dad, I want to take them by myself," said Dorie

"Why can't I tag along?" Paul asked.

"You could, but…" Dorie tried to finish.

Lynne nudged Paul, and a lightbulb lit up in Paul's head. He let out a great big laugh. "Oh, you want to see the horse, man." Lynne rolled her eyes.

"Come on, honey, we need to find you a hobby."

"Did you see what I did there? horse, man."

"Let's go, kids. Grandpa is silly." Dorie and the kids got to the stable. Max was there. He was talking to someone out of view.

As she got closer, Dorie noticed it was a woman that Max was talking to. The woman reached out and caressed Max's forearm.

Dorie's heart fell into her stomach. She felt sick, which was ridiculous. This man was nothing to her…her father's worker, her brother's friend. Dorie came into Max's view, and he moved away from the woman.

The woman looked at Dorie hard, said her goodbyes, and left.

"Dorie, I didn't know you were coming. I would have saddled up the horses," said Max.

"It's okay. The kids just wanted to visit the horses. I don't think riding is such a good idea," replied Dorie.

"Are you sure, beautiful riding weather? I can ride with Noah," Max continued.

"No, Really, just a visit. I'm not even sure why I came. You look like you were busy. We will just take a quick visit with the horses and be on our way. Thanks," Dorie's voice was suddenly flat, disinterested. Max felt like he had said something wrong.

"Okay," replied Max.

The kids went up and down the stables. Dorie followed them while Max hung back. Max had been trying to get up the nerve to ask Dorie out. Now, he was glad he waited. He could see she wasn't interested.

The time flew by, and it was time to get back to the house. Dorie got the kids buckled in, and she turned back. Max was watching her, and he looked so sad. I'm not here to get hurt with someone who's involved with another person, Dorie thought to herself as she gave Max a quick wave.

Dorie got back to the house. Of course, her father was in the parlor watching TV.

"Hi, honey. Did you have a good time?" Paul asked.

"It was okay, Dad. You can take the kids next time," Dorie replied.

"Dorie?" Paul tried to engage Dorie, but she didn't answer and just walked out of the room.

www.ingramcontent.com/pod-product-compliance
Lightning Source LLC
Chambersburg PA
CBHW040842010826
48978CB00012BB/868